Here Comes the Circus Train!

Written by Peter Trumbull
Illustrated by Lori Reiser

Toot, toot!

Look! Here comes the circus train. Can you hear the whistle blow?

The circus is coming
to our town. We will see
the three-ring show!

First the big blue engine
comes chugging
down the track.

The conductor rides
inside the cab as the train
goes "clickety-clack."

Next comes the mighty lion with his shaggy yellow mane.

Riding in his bright green car, he's king of the circus train.

Then comes a shiny
red car with the giraffe
so big and tall.

His long neck holds his head
so high, he looks
down to see us all.

Who is riding on the back and can wipe away your frown?

With a painted face
and a big red nose,
it must be the circus clown!

So step right up to
see the show before
the tent comes down.

We'll laugh and play
and cheer next time
the circus comes to town.